Summertime in the City

SHANI DENISE

ISBN: Electronic- 979-8-9997059-1-4
ISBN: Print - 979-8-9997059-0-7
Library of Congress Control Number: 2025916475

About the Author

Shani Denise writes soulful, spicy urban romances that explore Black love in all its beauty, mess, and magic. A Detroit native, she brings the city's grit and warmth to every page. She has a voice bold as her city and brings her characters to life with heart, heat, and healing.

Chapter 1

MEET ME AT THE CORNER STORE

Peaches

The Detroit heat was disrespectful that day.

It was past nine but still hot enough to melt the edge off my patience. My thighs stuck to the seat of my cousin's Cutlass like caramel on wax paper, and I was already irritated because the A/C hadn't worked since like '03. I told her I was only riding if we stopped at the corner store, and I meant it. I needed a cold-ass Faygo and a bag of Better Made chips before I snapped on somebody.

The corner store across from Save-a-lot on Houston Whittier was damn near empty, thank God. The old man behind the counter nodded at me like he always did—half bored, half suspicious.

I grabbed my Peach Faygo and some hot chips,

still fanning my neck with a wrinkled mail flyer. I was too focused on not sweating out my edges to notice him until I turned that corner by the cooler.

He had on a black A-shirt and some grey Nike shorts, bulky like he use to play on a DPS football team, tall as hell with this quiet energy like he ain't need to talk to be heard. His skin was a smooth, deep brown—sun-kissed and trouble. Tattoos crept up his arm like secrets.

And he looked right at me.

Not no creepy stare, not a "What's up my baby". Just a calm, bold look like... he recognized me, even though I knew we'd never met.

"You good?" he asked, voice low and soft but heavy, like bass you feel in your chest.

I blinked, caught off guard. "Huh? Yeah. It's just hot as hell."

He nodded, smirked a little. "You look like you 'bout to fight the sun."

I laughed before I could stop myself. "I am."

He leaned against the cooler like he had all night. "What's your name?"

I paused. Something about him made me want to lie. Say I was somebody different, somebody with less past. But I didn't."Peaches."

He smiled like the name tasted good in his mouth.

"For real?" he said. "That's your real name or your summer name?"

"Both," I said, lying just a little. "What about you?"

"Que."

Just Que. Like one syllable could carry all that quiet danger. I liked it. Way too much.

I tried to look away, but my body was already locked in. Something about him felt familiar—like a feeling I used to have before things got messy.

"You live around here?" he asked.

I shrugged. "Here and there. Auntie's house this week. Might be somewhere else by next."

He didn't push. Just nodded like he understood that kind of moving. That kind of life.

"You ever need somethin'," he said, stepping closer, "I be around. Look for the Impala sittin' low on 24s. Candy red."

I raised an eyebrow. "You giving me your car's description instead of your number?"

He grinned. "If you really wanna find me, you will."

Cocky. But not loud. Dangerous. But not reckless. My kinda mistake.

I didn't say nothing else, just paid for my stuff

and walked out, but I felt his eyes on me the whole way.

And as I slid back into that hot ass Cutlass, chips in my lap, Faygo sweating in my hand, I knew it already.

Umm Peaches… Peaches. My cousin snapped her fingers in front of my head. Hmm I said who was that nigga watching you like that. "Just some dude that was in the store."

I heard her mumble Hmmmhph sure!

But deep down I knew Que was gonna be my summertime problem.

Chapter 2

TALKIN' ON THE PORCH

Que

I wasn't even supposed to be on that side of town.

My cousin Jay had me ridin' shotgun through the east just to drop off some speakers he "forgot" to return to somebody who "don't need 'em no more." I didn't ask too many questions. I just kept the music low, one hand on the wheel, other hand thinkin' about her.

Peaches.

That name been in my head since the moment she walked out of the store. She moved like she knew people watched her—but didn't care. Her eyes were tired but still sharp. And that laugh? It hit something in me I forgot was even alive.

Ain't even been a full day, and she already had me doin' what I told myself I'd never do again—lookin' for somebody.

So I doubled back. Posted up outside my cuzzos on the east and waited for night to settle. Detroit nights always got that certain hum to 'em—like heat and tension sittin' right on top of your chest.

That's when I saw her again.

She was on the porch of a two-story house off the corner, legs crossed, bonnet on, licking red powder off her fingertips from them hot chips like she ain't just shifted my whole atmosphere yesterday.

I played it cool. Walked past slow. Didn't look directly, just nodded. She saw me though. I felt it in my bones.

"That the famous candy red Impala posted up over there?" she called out from her porch.

I stopped. Turned. Smiled.

"Yeah," I said. "That's my weekday ride. Weekend car in the shop."

She laughed and motioned for me to come up. Didn't ask who I was with or why I was on this block. Just invited me into her space like she knew I wasn't gonna bring no mess to it.

I took the bottom step. Sat down. Didn't wanna crowd her.

"You always out here solo?" I asked.

She shrugged. "Ain't too many people I like being around when I'm tryna think."

"What you thinking about?"

She looked at me long, like she was debating whether or not to lie.

"Leaving," she said finally. "Every summer I say I'ma dip. Go south or west. Just... go. But I never do."

I nodded slow. I knew that feeling too well. Wantin' to move but being stuck in place by roots you ain't even plant.

"What keeps you here?" I asked.

Her eyes dropped for a second. "Same thing that keeps everybody. Family, fear, fake love. "Take your pick."

Silence settled between us for a second. Not awkward. Just honest.

"I did a year upstate?" I said, not even knowin' why it came out.

She turned her head, and looked at me.

"Ok," she said. "Thanks for sayin' it like you ain't ashamed."

"I ain't," I said. "Wasn't proud of it either. But it happened. Came out quieter. Smarter."

She smiled at that. Real soft. And nodded.

"I like quiet," she said.

And just like that, we sat there. No more words. Her sipping Faygo through a straw, me watching the streetlights buzz like fake stars.

She ain't ask what I went in for.

I ain't ask what broke her before I came.

But somehow, I knew—we was both healing in places the world couldn't see. And maybe, just maybe, we wasn't meant to do that shit alone.

Peaches sat cross-legged, fanning herself. Her curls framed her face, looking beautiful with those glossy lips. Que leaned against the railing, watching her like she was the main event.

"You ever think about leavin'?" Peaches asked, not looking at him.

"Nah," Que said. "Detroit made me. Why would I leave the only place that ever showed me who I was?"

Peaches smiled. "That's the most poetic thing I've ever heard from a dude who drives an Impala with bullet holes."

They laughed, and something warm passed between them. Not heat from the heat, but that slow-burn type—intimate, dangerous, and soft all at once. Que inched closer, close enough to smell the peach oil on her skin.

"Why you really call me over here, Peaches?"

Her smile faded into something more vulnerable.

"Maybe I feel something that I'm not sure about yet and wondering if you feel the same?"

Que reached for her hand. "Depends. You really want to find out?"

Que

A slow silence wrapped around us, but it wasn't empty. It was heavy... full of all the things we weren't sayin'. Faintly hearing music playing from the cars cruising down the street, and the dice game happening on the corner. We sat still, feeling the night breeze envelop us.

P leaned back in the chair, her knees brushing mine just barely—soft. Her eyes stayed fixed on the street, but I could tell she was peeking at me in her periphery. Like she was curious... but cautious.

"You always this chill?" she asked.

I smirked. "Only when I'm not tryin' too hard."

She laughed low, a soft little hum in the back of her throat. That sound? It traveled down my spine and settled somewhere deep.

I shifted closer on the porch step, my arm brushing against hers now. She didn't move away.

"Can I tell you something?" I said.

She looked at me, slow. "You already told me you did a bid and got two cars. What else you got?"

I let a second pass.

"You got somethin' on your lips," I said.

Her brows lifted. She went to wipe it, but I stopped her.

"Nah. Let me."

I reached out—real slow, giving her time to pull back if she wanted. My thumb grazed the corner of her mouth, where a tiny smear of red powder lingered. Her breath hitched just a little.

But she didn't move.

Neither did I.

Her eyes met mine, and suddenly the air got thick. Her lips parted, not in surprise—in surrender.

I leaned in.

Slow.

Deliberate.

Like we both knew this was a turning point.

And when I kissed her... it wasn't wild or messy or rushed. It was soft, like summer wind on warm skin. Like two people saying, "I see you."

She kissed me back just as slow—no hunger, just heat. Her hand slid up the side of my face, her fingers light on my jaw, like she was memorizing me.

When we finally pulled apart, her eyes stayed closed for half a beat.

Then she whispered, "Damn, Que..."

I smiled, leaned back a little, heartbeat thudding slow but loud.

"Yeah, Damn."

Chapter 3

JUST VIBES

Peaches

After that kiss, Que didn't press me.

He didn't try to make it into a moment, didn't rush to follow it with more. He just leaned back on that porch like he'd been kissed by me before and knew he'd be kissed again.

And somehow, that made me wanna kiss him again even more.

But I played it cool.

The next night, he pulled up in the Impala—real low, real smooth—like he'd been driving slow on purpose, just in case I happened to be outside. And I was. Sitting on the porch, twisting and playing in my hair, hoping to see him again, hoping to feel his lips on mine.

"You hungry?" he asked, leaning out the window with that quiet smirk.

I was.

So we ended up on 7-mile and Hayes at Coney Time. He pulled up to the drive thru and ordered me a wingding dinner fried hard with chili cheese fries and a pink lemonade. I stared at him because there was no way he could've known what I ate here on the regular. We got our food and ate in the front seat, windows down, music low. Detroit summer songs playing from somebody else's block.

"How did you know my order?" I asked, I just figured he said with a shrug.

"You always this calm?" I asked, teasing.

He looked over at me, real still. "Not always. Just when I'm at peace.

"And I make you peaceful, huh?"

He smirked but didn't answer right away.

Then he said, "You don't make me peaceful. You remind me what it feels like."

Whew. I had to clench my thighs because this man gave me butterflies.

I looked away for a second, pretending I was real interested in the pigeons fighting over fries in the parking lot.

"You always been like this?" I asked. "All deep and mellow and mysterious?"

He laughed, head back a little. "Hell no. I used to be loud, angry, messy as hell. Thought I had somethin' to prove every time I stepped outside."

"So what changed?"

He went quiet for a second, staring at the steering wheel.

"My mama died while I was locked up. That changed everything."

I blinked. That hit harder than I expected. My chest got tight.

"I'm sorry," I said.

He nodded. "Ain't your fault. But it made me stop chasing all that noise. I just wanted peace. Quiet. A reason to keep going that wasn't rooted in pain.

That part stayed with me.

Because I knew that life. I been carrying my mama's absence like an extra rib since forever. My daddy wasn't around, and the women in my family only knew how to survive, and hustle—not love, not heal, just keep moving.

So when Que said that?

I felt him.

I reached over, laid my hand on his forearm. Didn't say a word. Didn't need to.

And he looked at me like nobody else had ever done before.

Not like I was broken or beautiful. Just real.

Like I could be both at the same time and he'd still choose me.

We sat there in that car for a long time, letting the city hum around us. He played me a few beats he'd been working on, told me how he used to make music before he got locked up.

"You ever think about doing it again?" I asked.

"Every day," he said. "But it's hard to chase dreams when life keeps draggin' you back to the block."

I looked at him.

"Then let's get off the block."

He smiled slow.

"That sound like an invitation?"

I grinned. "Might be."

Chapter 4

YOU GOT A SECRET OR SOMETHIN'?

Peaches

"You in love or just ducked off with somebody's daddy?"

That was the first thing my homegirl Nikki said when I finally showed up at her house on Saturday afternoon. She was sitting on her porch with a fresh face, lips full of lip gloss and a frozen cup in her hand, legs swinging like she was waiting to pop off.

Jazz was beside her, making her wig for the upcoming block party.

I rolled my eyes and flopped into a lawn chair.

"I ain't in love," I said, trying not to smile. "And definitely not with nobody's daddy."

"You stay disappearing," Nikki said, raising her brows. "Ever since that night at the corner store you've been different. I call, no answer. Text, no reply. Girl, you in a hostage situation?"

"Y'all dramatic," I said. But the truth sat sweet and low in my chest.

Because I had been gone.

Mentally and physically gone—somewhere else. Somewhere quieter. Softer. With Que.

We'd been posted up late in his car, talkin' and touchin' and just... being. No pressure, no fake performances. Just me and him. I'd forgotten what that felt like—being wanted for nothing but my presence.

Taking late night drives and having picnics on Belle Isle. We've been in our own bubble, and I wasn't ready to share that yet

"Her lips been extra glossy lately," Candice chimed in, chewing gum slow. "Somebody been getting kissed."

I laughed, but I felt heat rush to my cheeks.

"His name is Que dang," I said finally. "He low-key and were just getting to know each other. But he cool. Got me feelin'... I don't know. Like I can just be, like I can breathe around him."

Jazz gave me a look. "Girl, you sure he ain't married? Why are yall only hanging at night?"

"Were not. Just cus that's the only time yall see us don't mean that's what it is!

"You sure?"

"Stop playin'," I said, half laughing, half warning.

But Jazz sat up a little straighter. "Nah for real, where he from? You actin like we ain't all seen yo ex dudes like that before— You real quiet, and full of secrets."

I sucked my teeth. "It ain't like that."

They both went quiet, looking at me in that way only my girls could who have known me my whole life.

"Okay," Candice said finally. "Just don't go ghost on us over some porch-sitting, deep-talk-having jailbird with a pretty smile. You still got people that love you, Peaches."

That last part hit. Hard.

I nodded.

"I know," I said, quieter. "I'm just... figuring it out. He ain't like the others. And I ain't the same me no more either."

They looked at each other, then at me.

Jazz smirked, already knowing because out of everybody we go back to preschool. "Well, bring him to the block party. Let us judge for ourselves."

"Exactly," Nikki added. "If he got a good vibe, don't stare at Candice duck booty, and he can dance, I'll allow it."

I laughed again, but deep down, I knew I was nervous. My girls don't play about me and vice versa.

Because it was one thing to kiss somebody in the dark. It was another thing entirely to bring them into your world—with all its eyes, memories, and expectations.

Still... I texted Que that night.

Me: Block party on Alma tomorrow. Come thru.

Que: You want me there?

Me: Yeah. I do.

And just like that... the heat turned up.

Chapter 5

BLOCK PARTY BLUES

Que

The block on Alma was alive.

Grills smokin', speakers stacked on milk crates, kids runnin' wild with water guns and sticky fingers. Old heads domino slappin', aunties dancin' like they was 22 again. The whole street smelled like BBQ and liquor and secrets.

I pulled up slow, Impala glidin' over these speed-bumps. I spotted her in the crowd and she looked like she knew this wasn't just any pull-up. This was her block.

Peaches.

I hadn't even stepped out the car yet and already felt the eyes. Neighborhoods like this ain't forget faces — especially not new ones.

She spotted me from across the street, posted by a fold-out table with red cups and her girls flanking her like a security detail. Tight crop top, gold hoops, curls bouncin'. The whole block was hot, but she was the flame.

"Que!" she called out, waving me over like I belonged there. I didn't. But I walked over anyway.

Her girls who she introduced as Nikki and Jazz looked me up and down like TSA. I gave a small nod, dap'd the dude next to me, and kept my eyes on Peaches.

"You good?" I asked, leaning in just enough to smell the peach lip gloss. Kissing her gently behind her ear. Smelling the real fruit, real temptation.

"I'm good," she said, smirking. "Was starting to think you'd punk out."

"Punk out of what?"

"Meetin' my whole block."

I chuckled. "You set me up."

"Yup."

Before I could reply, some tall dude in a Tigers jersey came up from behind her, all chest and memory.

"Aye, Peach," he said, loud on purpose. "Thought you said you ain't messin' with no more hood dudes?"

Peaches stiffened. "Keep it movin', Meech."

I stayed calm, didn't flex or puff my chest. Just stood beside her, quiet but present. He looked me over like he wanted a reason. I didn't give him one.

"You Que, huh?" Meech said, eyes narrowing.

I didn't smile. "You tryna ask, or tryna start somethin'?"

Peaches stepped between us fast. "Chill. Both of y'all."

Meech laughed it off, backed away. "Just sayin', Peach. Be careful who you bring 'round here. Not everybody who smile in your face got good intentions."

"Like you huh? She said."

And just like that, she grabbed my hand and led me thru the crowd. The music was still bumpin', but the air got thick.

I looked at her. "He used to be somebody?"

"He used to be nobody," she said. "But he don't like lettin' go."

"You want me to leave?"

She paused. That long pause where pride and vulnerability fight it out.

Then she finally replied. "No. I want you to dance with me."

I blinked. "For real?"

"Yup."

She grabbed my hand, pulled me toward the center of the street where people were already moving. Summer Walker turned into some old 90s R&B joint, and before I knew it, her hips were pressed into mine, slow and easy.

"I don't really dance," I said low in her ear.

"You don't have to," she whispered back. "Just feel me, Hold me."

So I did.

Right there on Alma, with eyes watching, I let my hands rest on her waist and moved with her like we'd been moving together all our lives.

All I could think was:

Damn.

This girl could make me forget my past.

Or maybe... she was about to become my future.

Chapter 6

THIS AIN'T JUST HEAT

Peaches

The next day, the block was quiet.

Party over. Bottles in recycling bins. Folding chairs flipped over like the night got too wild. And me? I was hiding in my auntie's upstairs window, watching Que pull up and sit in the car.

He ain't text.

Just sat.

Like he was waiting to see if I'd come down. Like he didn't wanna press, but he wasn't gonna pretend nothing had shifted either.

'Cause something had.

I ain't even know what it was, exactly. Just… this feeling. Like the closer he got, the more I felt parts of me I'd buried deep start to rise.

Parts that wanted something real. Something stable. Something I never believed could last. Love…

And that scared the hell outta me.

Nikki's voice echoed in my head. "You sure he ain't just a summer vibe?"

That's the thing. I didn't know. It felt like more, but what if it wasn't? What if I let him all the way in just for him to dip once the leaves turned?

Detroit had a way of makin' things feel deeper than they really were. The city could wrap you in heat, throw music in the air, give you somebody fine and flawed to hold for a little while — and then poof. September hits and folks vanish like smoke.

I finally came downstairs, slow, like I didn't know he was out there.

He rolled the window down. "You good?"

I nodded. "You tryna talk?"

"Always."

I slid into the passenger seat. We sat in silence for a second, just the hum of the engine between us.

Then I said it.

"Is this real for you, Que? Or we just two people tryna survive the summer?"

He looked at me hard. Not angry. Just real.

"You think I waste time like this with people I don't feel?"

"I don't know what you do," I said, voice tight. "I don't know if I'm something new or just... something for now."

He didn't answer right away. Just turned the engine off, leaned back in the seat.

"You ever been with somebody who made you feel calm inside?" he asked. "Like... not hyped up, not nervous, just seen?"

I didn't answer.

"That's what this is for me," he said, eyes on the windshield. "I ain't out here playin'. You could be just a summer vibe—but I don't want you to be."

Silence again.

Then I whispered, "I'm scared it won't last."

He turned to me, hand reaching for mine.

"Then let's stop lookin' at the end and just be in it. Right here. Right now."

I looked down at our fingers intertwined.

And for the first time in a long time, I didn't feel like running.

The Fourth of July fireworks is falling on Juneteenth this year and Que planned a picnic date for us.

Babe today has been amazing. I said kissing and sucking on his bottom lip. He returned by nip on my chin. As night crept up on us so did his hands around my waist holding me and caressing me with love. Was this love? Before I could analyze my thoughts, the sky lit up with bursts of red, white, and gold. Kids screamed, grills smoked, and bass thumped from cars creeping by. We sat on the hood of his Impala, with my favorite bottle of peach Faygo between us.

"You know," Peaches said, "you never told me what your dream is."

Que leaned back, watching the sky explode. "To have something that don't gotta be hidden or hustled. Something I don't gotta lie to keep."

Peaches looked over. "Like this?"

He nodded. "Exactly like this."

She rested her head on his shoulder. The night wrapped around them like a secret they didn't mind the world knowing.

"Summertime in the city," she whispered. "Nothing has ever felt this good."

Chapter 7

WHERE MUSIC LIVES

Que

I don't bring nobody to the studio.

Ain't even a real studio — just a back room in my cousin's basement with foam on the walls and an old MPC that still knock if you treat her right. But to me, it's sacred. It's where I talk to myself in sounds, where I let out shit I don't got words for.

Tonight, I brought Peaches.

She walked in slow, eyes wide like a kid in a candy store, brushing her fingers over the dusty keyboard and old mic stand. She ain't say nothin' at first. Just looked around like she could feel the weight of everything that ever happened in this space.

"You made all this?" she asked, voice soft.

"Every sound in here came from me," I said. "Even the pain."

She turned toward me; arms wrapped across her chest.

"I been wantin' to see this side of you."

"You sure?"

"'Cause once you hear me in here," I said, motioning toward the booth, "you'll know too much."

She smiled, stepped closer. "I wanna know."

I sat down at the board, pressed play on a track I never let anybody hear before. Just keys at first. Melancholy, then warm. A low hum of bass. Then a voice — mine — coming in slow, not rapping, but saying something.

"Ain't no silence like the kind after love."

"Ain't no noise louder than your own thoughts."

"But I still wait for a voice that sound like peace."

Peaches closed her eyes while it played. She didn't talk. Didn't move. Just listened.

When it faded out, she came to stand behind me, wrapped her arms around my shoulders from behind. Her cheek pressed against the back of my neck, soft and warm.

"Que..." she whispered.

I turned the chair. She was right there, close.

"Why me?" she asked, voice barely audible. "Why you openin' up to me like this?"

I searched her face — eyes that had seen too much, lips that smiled through pain, a body that carried grace and fire.

"'Cause you real," I said. "And when I'm with you, I feel like I ain't just surviving. I'm... alive."

Her lips parted slightly, like she wanted to speak but couldn't find the words.

So, I kissed her.

Not rushed.

Not like the porch.

But slow and full. The kind that says, "I mean this."

Her hands found my chest, my shoulders, my jaw — like she needed to touch every part of me to believe I was real.

We moved together like we'd done before in another life. She climbed into my lap, straddling me in that creaky old studio chair, both of us wrapped in shadows and basslines.

And at that moment, it wasn't just about bodies. It was about safety.

About finally letting somebody see you and not flinch.

Peaches

His lips were on mine, soft and sure.

There wasn't no rush in him. Just warmth. Just time. Like he'd been waiting for this moment—not to get what he wanted, but to give me what I needed.

His kiss moved slow down my neck, hands gliding up my sides, fingertips barely brushing the skin beneath my shirt like I was something fragile. He looked at me the whole time, searching my face for a sign — Yes, or no?

I gave it. Not with words. With the way I held his face and pulled him into me.

"Come here," I whispered.

He lifted me like I weighed nothing, carried me over to the futon in the corner of the studio. The room was dim, lit only by the glow from the mixing board and a blue lava lamp in the back that made everything feel like a dream.

I pulled his shirt over his head — slow — eyes tracing the tattoos across his chest, inked with stories he hadn't told me yet. He watched me do it like I was the only person who'd ever looked at him like that. Like he wasn't just a body. Like he was a man I saw, fully.

"You sure?" he asked again, his voice hoarse.

I nodded, then said, "I want to remember what it feels like to be touched and not torn."

His jaw clenched.

And then he touched me — like a promise.

Not one rough move. Not one greedy hand. Just skin to skin, breath to breath. He undressed me like he was learning me, like each layer he peeled away told him something new.

By the time he was inside me, I had already given him everything.

He moved with me slow, deep, steady. One hand in my hair, the other holding my thigh like he was grounding us both. We didn't speak. Didn't moan like we were on some movie screen. We just breathed each other in. Let the silence fill with feeling.

At one point, I looked up at him, tears sitting heavy in my eyes for no damn reason.

He kissed my cheek, then my shoulder, then said low, "You safe here, Peach. You home."

That did it.

I wrapped my arms around him and let go — of the fear, the walls, the weight I'd been carrying since I was too young to name it.

We moved slow like time had stretched just for us.

And when we both finally came down, wrapped up in each other, heartbeats crashing soft and quiet like waves… I knew. This wasn't just summer. It was real.

Chapter 8

STILL HERE

Que

The air hit different in Detroit; fall was on the horizon.

The air was cooler. Quieter. The street noise felt less like celebration, more like survival again. That golden-hour glow that came with summer had faded into soft gray mornings and real-life decisions.

And the nights?

They felt like countdowns.

Peaches got a job offer in Atlanta. Her cousin Arie and Tahitia ran a boutique down there and said they could use help setting up a new store. "Temporary," she told me. "Just for a few months to stack, and a change in scenery."

But I knew what that really meant.

It was a door.

One I didn't wanna close... but didn't know how to walk through either.

We sat in the Impala one last time outside her auntie's house. Hoodie on. Her curls tied up, but edges still perfect. She wasn't dressed like summer anymore. She was dressed like change.

"You mad at me?" she asked, eyes on the street.

"Nah," I said. "You gotta move. I respect that."

"But?"

"But I'd be lyin' if I said it don't feel like the end."

She looked at me, long and real. "What we had this summer... it felt like a movie."

"It was real, it was a vibe."

"I know," she whispered. "But life don't care about vibes."

I stayed quiet.

I wanted to say, "Come back after." I wanted to say, "I'll come, or I'll visit." But I'd made promises like that before. They don't always hold up.

So instead I asked, "You ever think about staying?"

She didn't answer right away.

"I did. Every day," she said finally. "But I been

staying for everybody else my whole life. This time…
I gotta choose me.”

That hurt.

But I understood it too deep to be bitter.

I reached for her hand. “So, what we doin’?”

She squeezed back. “We hold onto what we got. If it’s real, it won’t disappear just ‘cause summer’s over.”

“And if it don’t hold?”

“Then at least we gave it all we had. No regrets.”

She kissed me slow. Not like the first time. Not like the studio. Not the countless times this summer. But like a goodbye that wasn’t really a goodbye. We didn’t have to say I love you because we felt it.

Then she slid out the car.

And I watched her walk up those porch steps without looking back. A part of me wanted to be selfish and tell her not to leave but I couldn’t. I needed her to see what was out there past these city limits. Some people never ventured past 8-mile their whole lives, I wanted her to not have regrets.

I rolled the window down “Stay the night with me.” She halted turning slowly like she was weighing her options. She was biting her lip while shaking her head no while whispering ok. The rain started as we rode to my apartment.

The rain tapped slow against the windows of Que's apartment—thick summer droplets that cooled the city, but not the heat rising between them.

Peaches stood at the foot of his bed in an oversized T-shirt that clearly wasn't hers. Que leaned against the doorframe, a towel slung low on his hips from the shower, chest still damp.

"You always lookin' at me like that," she said, biting her lip.

"Like what?"

"Like you tryna learn me with your eyes."

"That's 'cause I am, he murmured, walking toward her. Tryna memorize everything... before it changes."

She softened. "You scared it will?"

"I'm scared it already has."

She pulled him down by the towel, lips brushing his jaw. "Then don't talk. Just touch me."

Que obeyed.

His hands slid under the T-shirt, finding bare skin and curves that only he got to worship. Their mouths met in a kiss that was less hungry this time, more aching. Like they were loving with urgency, but also reverence.

He laid her down slow, kissed every inch like a prayer—neck, collarbone, soft places that made her whimper. Her nails raked his back, pulling him deeper into her heat, her heartbeat, her truth.

There was no rush. No game. Just sweat and slow thrusts and whispered names between shaky breaths.

"Tell me I'm yours," she whispered.

"You been mine," he answered, moving inside her like he meant it. "Every damn day since I saw you at that corner store."

She smiled against his lips, tears mixing with sweat. "Then stay in this moment with me. Just tonight."

Que made love to her, squeezing her, holding her tighter, willing his mind not to think about her leaving. He made passionate love to her over and over again. Giving her his all, saying to her what he desperately wanted to say through every thrust, lick, position, and moan. He was moving as if the world outside didn't exist and as if reality would come in the morning.

"I ain't goin' nowhere," he whispered, even if they both knew life had other plans.

Chapter 9

HOMESICK

Peaches

It's been six weeks.

Atlanta's hot but it isn't home.

I'm working. I'm learning. I'm growing. But I still hear his voice sometimes when I close my eyes. Still feel his touch when the world gets too loud.

Sometimes I wonder if I'll go back.

Sometimes I wonder if he's waiting.

But most days, I don't wonder — I know.

Because something about Que... wasn't temporary.

It was rooted.

And love that's rooted?

It don't die with summer.

I was so homesick and thinking about Que but

never picked up the phone. Telling myself its easier if we don't talk. I felt like I was physically sick, but I told myself it was just the change of weather and atmosphere. Fall had crept in and the chill in the air was taking over. Working in my cousin's boutique was decent but nothing felt like home. Not the clubs, not the food, not the atmosphere.

It had been weeks, and I still didn't feel like myself. Talking on the phone with my girls Tina, Nene, and Candi they joked that I wasn't just sick from missing home but probably pregnant. Zoning out I asked myself when was my last period? I couldn't remember, shaking my head naw, that couldn't be it, could it? Waiting another couple days I finally coerced myself into buying a test. It was the test I almost didn't take.

I'd been tired. Sick to my stomach. Nerves buzzing like I drank too much coffee, but I hadn't touched caffeine in weeks. I thought maybe it was stress. Moving. Working nonstop.

But the second that little line showed up, everything went quiet.

And in that silence… I knew.

I was pregnant.

I stared at the bathroom mirror in my cousin's guest room, heart pacing like a race I hadn't trained for. I wasn't scared. Not like I expected it to be. I was… still, quiet.

Looking in that mirror I saw myself different. Stronger. Softer. Wiser.

I knew what and who I wanted and what I needed.

Chapter 10

DETROIT BOUND

Peaches

And then, like instinct, like muscle memory—I packed a bag, booked a one-way ticket, to go home. I was coming back to Detroit, but would he want us? Did he move on? I had so many questions. Did he feel the same and the only way to find out was to go to him.

I didn't call Que.

Didn't text him.

Just showed up.

He was working on his car when I pulled up in the Uber. Hoodie on, hands greasy, music bumpin' low from his speaker on the porch. He didn't see me right away. Not until I said his name.

He turned around slow, eyes landing on me like he wasn't sure I was real.

"Peaches?" he said, stepping closer.

I nodded, heart thudding. "I came back."

"For good?" he asked, cautious but hopeful.

I stepped forward, took his hand, and laid it on my stomach.

His whole body froze.

"You serious?" he whispered.

I nodded, voice cracking. "I found out last week. I didn't want to tell you over the phone. I wanted to come home."

He didn't say anything. Just pulled me into him, wrapped both arms around me like I might float away if he let go.

"You good with this?" I whispered against his chest.

"I Love You P, I should've told you sooner! Should've followed you Baby.

"I'm ready for this," he said. "You. Us. The baby. All of it."

I let myself cry for real this time.

Because in this moment I realized that this wasn't just a summer thing anymore.

This was life.

This was family.

This was a love made in summertime in the city.

-The End-

Epilogue

JUST US, FOREVER

Our baby boy was asleep, soft breaths rising and falling in the bassinet beside the couch. The whole house smelled like vanilla, lavender and warm bottles. Outside, Detroit was quiet—just past midnight, the city finally exhaling.

Peaches stood in the kitchen in one of Que's Tshirts, her curls wild from the shower, a mug of tea in her hand.

"You look good in my shirt," Que said from the doorway, eyes low and loving.

She smirked. "Boy, hush."

But he didn't move. Just watched her like he had a question buried deep behind his ribcage.

"What?" she asked, sipping.

"You ever think about how we got here?" he said, voice low. "Started on a porch. Now you here, makin' tea, our baby snorin' two feet away."

She leaned on the counter, teasing, "Wasn't exactly the plan."

He walked toward her. Slow. Steady. And when he reached her, he dropped to one knee.

Her breath caught.

He pulled a ring from his pocket—simple, classic, silver band with a single diamond that sparkled like sunlight off Belle Isle's water.

"No speech," he said. "No big moment. Just this. Me and you here in the quiet. Been through hell, through heatwaves, heartbreaks… and we still here."

She blinked, tears slipping without warning.

"Marry me, Peaches. Be my wife. Let's continue building this for Forever."

She covered her mouth, nodding before she could even get the words out.

"Yes," she whispered, dropping to her knees in front of him. "Yes. Que, yes."

He slipped the ring on her finger with shaking hands, and they held each other like they were making another vow—no matter how wild the world got, they would always choose each other.

Always.